Going Places
with Rosy Rabbit

by Robin Edward
illustrated by Pat Reynolds

Harcourt
SCHOOL PUBLISHERS

Printed in China

ISBN 10: 0-15-351353-5
ISBN 13: 978-0-15-351353-4

Ordering Options
ISBN 10: 0-15-351211-3 (Grade 1 Advanced Collection)
ISBN 13: 978-0-15-351211-7 (Grade 1 Advanced Collection)
ISBN 10: 0-15-358039-9 (package of 5)
ISBN 13: 978-0-15-358039-0 (package of 5)

4 5 6 7 8 9 10   0940   15 14 13 12 11 10 09

When Rosy Rabbit climbed inside the box, it felt just right. Rosy said to her sisters, "I'm going to drive this bus all over the earth. Watch me go!" She put on her cap and off she went.

2

She drove around bends and over
bumps, up hills and beside trees.
Then she went by some houses—
and there were her sisters!

"Stop!" they cried. "We want
a ride!"

3

Her sisters climbed in.

"Go, bus, go!" said Rosy.

Around all the streets, she drove the bus. Some of her sisters got off at the shops. Some got off at the railroad stop.

4

"A bus is too slow," said Rosy,
and she pulled off her cap. "Go, train,
go!" she said.

Chug chug, the train started.
Then off it went, down the track
so fast that the smoke went in
Rosy's eyes.

"Wait for us!" cried her sisters.

"We thought you might not stop!"
they said.

"I'm going to a cold place now,"
said Rosy. "I'm sailing a ship where
there's ice in the sea. It's cold all day
and all night."

Her sisters snuggled up close.

"I'm just fooling you!" cried Rosy.
"This is not a boat in a cold place."
She pulled down the sail. "This is a
truck in the jungle. We have to go
slowly because of the mud—and
there's a beast creeping up on us!"

"Oh, no!" cried her sisters.

"Oh, yes!" said their mother.

"You gave us a fright!" said the sisters. "We thought you were the beast!"

"We drove to places all over the earth," said Rosy.

"Then you must want a sandwich," smiled Mother.

Rosy Rabbit put on the brake right away. She stopped by the table. "We do," she said. "Seeing all these places has made us need some food!"